Lila's loneliest day . . .

"I don't want a nanny!" I yelled as we went upstairs.

Daddy took me into my room. "You can come out when you calm down," he told me. Then he went into the hallway and closed the door behind him.

I stood staring at the door.

Mommy was gone.

Daddy didn't love me enough to take care of me himself.

My parents were getting divorced.

My friends would never understand.

I was totally alone.

I threw myself on my bed and started to sob.

Bantam Books in the SWEET VALLEY KIDS series

SWEET VALLEY KIDS

LILA'S CHRISTMAS ANGEL

Written by
Molly Mia Stewart

Created by
FRANCINE PASCAL

Illustrated by
Ying-Hwa Hu

BANTAM BOOKS
NEW YORK · TORONTO · LONDON · SYDNEY · AUCKLAND

RL 2, 005-008

LILA'S CHRISTMAS ANGEL
A Bantam Book / December 1995

*Sweet Valley High® and Sweet Valley Kids® are
registered trademarks of Francine Pascal*

Conceived by Francine Pascal

*Produced by Daniel Weiss Associates, Inc.
33 West 17th Street
New York, NY 10011*

Cover art by Susan Tang

ISBN: 0-553-48216-5

Published simultaneously in the United States and Canada

*Bantam Books are published by Bantam Books, a division of Bantam
Doubleday Dell Publishing Group, Inc. Its trademark, consisting of the
words "Bantam Books" and the portrayal of a rooster, is Registered in the
U.S. Patent and Trademark Office and in other countries. Marca
Registrada. Bantam Books, 1540 Broadway, New York, New York 10036.*

PRINTED IN THE UNITED STATES OF AMERICA

OPM   0 9 8 7 6 5 4 3 2 1

To Ryan Lee Vandersloot

CHAPTER 1

Holiday Blues

Hello! I'm Lila Fowler. I'm going to to tell you a wonderful story about how I met my guardian angel.

I know what you're thinking. You don't believe in angels. But *you* have a guardian angel, too! Everyone does. If you ever need her your angel will be watching over you. I promise!

I met my guardian angel just before Christmas. If she hadn't appeared, Christmas would have been the loneliest day in my whole life.

But before I can tell you about

Serena—that's my guardian angel—I have to tell you about me.

I'm seven years old. My eyes are brown, and my hair is long and dark. I usually wear it back in a headband. I have about fifty different kinds.

My dad owns a business. He drives a fancy car with a phone in it. Daddy is one of the most important men in Sweet Valley (that's the town where we live). He's also rich. That's what my friends tell me.

Our house is one of the biggest in the whole town. My room is huge—I can turn eight cartwheels in a row without hitting a wall. On one end of my room there's a gigantic closet, stuffed full of clothes. I wear a different outfit every day. I get a new toy at the mall every Saturday. Dolls are my favorites. They all live in my dollhouse, because it's big enough for a million dolls to live in!

I'm in the second grade at Sweet Valley Elementary School. My teacher is Mrs. Otis. She's nice. I sit between my two best friends in class. Their names are Ellen Riteman and Jessica Wakefield.

Ellen and Jessica like to play with dolls and wear pretty clothes, just like I do. We all hate boys. On the playground, we like to jump rope, play hopscotch, or swing on the swings. Jessica wants to be an actress when she grows up. Ellen wants to be an archaeologist. I'd like to be the queen of an enormous country.

Sometimes people call Jessica "Elizabeth" by mistake. That's because Jessica and Elizabeth look exactly alike. They are identical twins. They both have blond hair and blue eyes. But even though a lot of people can't tell the twins apart, I never confuse them. They *act* totally different.

If you ask me, Jessica is lots more fun. She likes to play practical jokes. And she doesn't worry about hurting people's feelings all the time.

Elizabeth isn't half as much fun. She's a goody-goody. She likes absolutely *everybody*. Even boys! I'm nice to Elizabeth, but only because Jessica gets mad when I make fun of her.

Even though I think Elizabeth is boring, I am jealous of Jessica sometimes. I wish I had a twin sister. Or just a regular sister, like Ellen has.

I'm an only child. It gets lonely without anyone to play with at home. And holidays are the loneliest times of all! I got so lonely at Christmastime that my guardian angel had to rescue me. . . .

"This one is for you!" Jessica smiled as she handed me a small red envelope.

"Thanks," I mumbled.

Jessica turned to Ellen and gave her an identical envelope. "And this one is for you!" she said.

Jessica, Ellen, and I were sitting at our desks at school. Class hadn't started yet.

Elizabeth was walking around the room. She was handing out an entire stack of little red envelopes.

"What is it?" Ellen asked as she looked at her envelope. She sounded excited.

"Open it and see," Jessica said.

"But it's addressed to me and Mommy," Ellen pointed out. "I should take it home so we can open it together."

I glanced at my envelope. In Jessica's handwriting, it read, *Lila and Mrs. Fowler.*

"If you won't open your invitations, I'll tell you about it," Jessica said.

"We're having a cookie party!"

"What's a cookie party?" Ellen asked.

Elizabeth skipped up to us. She sat down at her desk on Jessica's other side. She leaned forward so she could see Ellen and me.

"Before the party each family will bake a batch of cookies," Jessica explained. "They'll bring the cookies to the party."

"At the party, we'll all trade," Elizabeth put in. "Everyone will go home with a plate of mixed holiday cookies."

"Will we get to eat any cookies at the party?" Ellen asked.

"Hundreds!" Elizabeth said.

"Thousands!" Jessica said.

"Millions!" Elizabeth said.

Ellen giggled. "That sounds like fun. Christmas cookies are yummy."

I looked down at my invitation. The words "Lila and Mrs. Fowler" got

blurry. I bit my bottom lip to keep from crying. I did not want anyone to see me cry.

Jessica and Elizabeth didn't know that Mommy had moved out of our house a few days earlier. She'd left Sweet Valley. She was not coming back.

Mommy and Daddy were getting divorced. That meant they wouldn't be married anymore. They both said their decision had nothing to do with me—it was because of adult arguments.

I missed Mommy. I'd been sad and lonely ever since she'd left. Daddy was always so busy working that he never had any time to spend with me.

But one thing *was* better since Mommy had left. I didn't have to listen to angry yelling anymore. Mommy and Daddy had fought every night for months. I hate yelling.

Now our house was nice and quiet.

Sometimes I was happy about the divorce. Sometimes it made me mad. But most of the time I just didn't know what to think. There was only one thing I knew for sure: I didn't want my friends to know Mommy had left. All of them had a mother and a father. They wouldn't like me if I was different. They would just think I was weird.

"Aren't you going to open your invitation?" Elizabeth asked me.

"No."

Elizabeth looked worried. I didn't want her to know I was upset. Once she knew that, she would try to figure out *why*.

I forced myself to smile. "I want to open the invitation with Mommy," I told Elizabeth. "It's addressed to her, too."

"That sounds nice," Elizabeth said.

My heart was beating fast. I was happy I had fooled Elizabeth. But she had come close to guessing something was bothering me.

I was not happy about the party. When Mommy didn't show up, the twins would know something was wrong.

I had to stop the cookie party.

But how?

CHAPTER 2

A Close Call

"**I** have something to tell you," I whispered to Jessica the next morning on the playground. We were waiting for a turn on the swings. Amy Sutton, Elizabeth, and Ellen were already swinging, and Caroline Pearce was ahead of us in line.

"What is it?" Jessica asked.

"A secret," I said. "I can't tell you here."

"Can't tell her what?" Caroline demanded. She always has to know everything. And she doesn't even *try* to keep secrets.

Jessica stuck her tongue out at Caroline. "Mind your own beeswax," she said. "Come on, Lila. Let's go somewhere we can be alone."

"Let's go over by the water fountain," I suggested. "Nobody is there now."

"OK," Jessica said.

I wasn't surprised she had agreed. Jessica loves secrets. She can never resist hearing one.

"I don't care about your stupid secret, anyway," Caroline called after us as we walked away.

"Good," Jessica called back. "Because you're never going to hear it!"

I followed Jessica across the playground. My stomach was going flip-flop-flip. My hands were sweaty.

"What's the secret?" Jessica asked when we got to the water fountain.

I took a deep breath. "Nobody wants to come to your party," I said.

"Why?" Jessica asked, her eyes widening.

I shrugged. "Everyone thinks it's a silly idea."

Jessica's bottom lip started to quiver.

I stared down at my shoes, feeling awful. I had made up the lie so Jessica would call off her party. But I didn't want to make her cry.

"If you want, I'll tell everyone the party's off," I mumbled.

Before Jessica could answer, Eva Simpson ran up to the water fountain.

I usually like Eva. She is from Jamaica. Her clothes are really cool. But at that moment I wasn't too happy to see her.

Eva took a long drink of water. As she wiped her mouth, she turned to Jessica. "I can't wait for your party," she said. "It's going to be so much fun! I'm bringing Daddy."

"You're coming?" Jessica sounded surprised.

"Sure," Eva said. "Everyone is going to be there."

Jessica looked at me. Her lips were pressed tightly together. She put her hands on her hips.

"Um—I've got to go," I said.

"Oh, no, you don't!" Jessica put out a hand to stop me. "You're a liar!"

"What's wrong?" Eva asked.

Suddenly I saw a flash of white. It looked like a very large bird fluttering by. The flash lasted only a second. When it was over, I looked back at Jessica. She was smiling.

"Aren't you mad at me?" I asked.

"Why would I be mad?" Jessica asked. "Your joke about the party was funny!"

I frowned. What had made Jessica change her mind so quickly? Did it have something to do with the white flash?

"Do you guys want to play tag?" Eva asked. She's a tomboy, like Elizabeth.

Jessica wrinkled her nose. "No, thanks."

I noticed Jessica and Eva weren't talking about the flash. Had they even seen it?

"Want to swing on the swings?" Eva asked.

"OK," Jessica agreed. "Come on, Lila!"

The three of us ran across the playground. The line for the swings was gone. We each grabbed a swing.

I still wasn't sure what the white flash had been. But I was glad it had stopped me from having a fight with Jessica.

I didn't want to start fighting with my friends. That would just make me even more lonely. I decided not to try to stop the cookie party anymore.

"I can go higher than you!" Eva yelled.

"Cannot!" Jessica shouted.

Eva and Jessica started to push their swings higher and higher.

I didn't push my swing very hard. *What will I say when the twins ask why Mommy isn't at their party?* I wondered. Maybe I could say she was in Hollywood for a screen test. Or that she had joined the circus. Or become an astronaut.

I hadn't talked to Mommy since she had left. I didn't even know where she was.

Maybe one of those things is even true, I thought sadly.

CHAPTER 3

An Awful Surprise

"Hi, Lila," Daddy said that afternoon as I climbed into his shiny green car. "How was school today?"

"Awful," I said in a grumpy voice. I didn't want Daddy to pick me up at school. All of my friends knew Mommy used to do that. What if they saw Daddy? They might guess something was wrong.

"Did you learn anything interesting?" Daddy asked.

"Not really," I said with a shrug. I didn't feel like telling Daddy I'd finally learned to make my cursive capital *E*'s perfectly. Or that I had got a B+ on my math worksheet. Mommy was the one who knew how hard I had to work at writing cursive. And Mommy was the one who knew I usually got A's in math. Daddy wouldn't really care, I thought.

"I have a surprise waiting for you at home," Daddy said.

"Is it Mommy?" I asked right away.

"No, it's not Mommy," Daddy said. He sounded tired.

"Then what is it?" I asked.

"You'll see when we get home," Daddy answered.

I started to feel a tiny bit less grumpy. I absolutely adore surprises. I could hardly wait to get home. When Daddy finally pulled up in front of our house, I jumped out of the car.

"Come on," I said, pulling on Daddy's hand. "Show me my surprise!"

Daddy laughed. "Right this way," he said.

Holding my hand, Daddy led me into our kitchen. A woman was sitting at the table.

"Who's she?" I asked.

"She's your surprise," Daddy told me.

"Hi!" The woman stood up and held a hand out to me. "I'm Harriet. I hope we can be good friends."

I put my hands behind my back and gave her an angry look.

Harriet was dressed in a sweatshirt and sneakers. *What a messy person,* I thought. She had black hair that came down all the way to her waist—fun hair to braid. *But I don't want to play with it,* I told myself.

"Harriet is going to be your nanny," Daddy told me. "She'll be cooking for you, driving you to school, and helping you with your homework."

"But Mommy does those things," I said.

Harriet wasn't holding out her

hand anymore. She was still smiling, but she did not really look happy.

"Lila," Daddy said softly. "You know your mommy isn't here anymore. She can't do those things for you now."

"I don't need a nanny," I said. "I don't want a nanny, and I'm not going to have one!"

"Lila," Daddy said in a warning voice.

"You can go home now," I told Harriet.

"This *is* my home," Harriet said.

Daddy tried to make me look at him, but I pushed him away.

"I know you'd rather have your mommy here," Daddy said. "But I think you'll like Harriet very much."

"No!" I yelled, stomping my foot as hard as I could.

"Lila!" Daddy said.

Harriet knelt down next to me. "I promise we'll have lots of fun together—"

"Get away from me!" I screamed. "I

don't like you. You look like a witch!"

Daddy reached down and grabbed my hand. "That's enough out of you, young lady," he said sharply.

Harriet looked sad as she watched Daddy lead me out of the kitchen. But I was not fooled into thinking she cared about me.

"I don't want a nanny!" I yelled as we went up the stairs.

Daddy took me into my room. "You can come out when you calm down," he told me. Then he went into the hallway and closed the door behind him.

I stood staring at the door.

Mommy was gone.

Daddy didn't love me enough to take care of me himself.

My parents were getting divorced.

My friends would never understand.

I was totally alone.

I threw myself onto my bed and started to sob.

CHAPTER 4

An Angel Without Wings

I was still lying in bed when I heard a sweet voice say, "Don't cry."

Surprised, I looked up. I'd thought I was all alone. Who could be in my bedroom?

A girl I'd never seen before was sitting at the foot of my bed. She had huge green eyes and very light blond hair. She was wearing a flowing white dress.

"Who are you?" I asked.

"My name is Serena," the girl said. "I'm your guardian angel."

"My *what*?" I asked.

"Your guardian angel," Serena repeated.

I didn't believe it. I sat up and crossed my arms. I thought Serena—if that was really her name—was playing a joke on me. And I was in no mood for jokes.

"If you're an angel, prove it," I said. "Fly!"

Serena sighed. "I wish I could. I think flying must be the most wonderful thing in the universe! But I can't fly. I don't have my wings yet."

"Then grant me three wishes." I was already thinking about what I'd wish for.

"I'm not a genie," Serena said. "I can't grant wishes. I'm an angel. I do good deeds."

"So do one," I said.

"OK." Serena thought for a moment. "Harriet has a headache. I'll get rid of it."

Now if Harriet had a headache, I considered it *good* news. I would have liked her to keep it forever. But it didn't seem right to admit that to someone who might be an angel.

"Come on," Serena said.

When she stood up, my heart started to beat faster. Standing in front of me, Serena seemed to float above the ground. For the first time, I wondered if she really could be an angel.

Serena floated out of my room and down the hall.

"Won't Harriet wonder who you are?" I asked as I hurried after her.

"No," Serena replied. "I'm *your* guardian angel. You are the only one who can see and hear me."

Serena opened the door to one of the guest bedrooms. A suitcase was lying on the bed. *If Serena isn't an angel, how does she know which room is*

Harriet's? I wondered. Even I didn't know that.

"Careful," Serena told me when we reached the bathroom door. "Don't let Harriet see you."

Serena went into the bathroom. I peeked around the door frame.

Harriet was lying in a bubble bath with her eyes closed. She was frowning and rubbing her head.

Serena waved her hand.

Harriet smiled. The little wrinkles on her forehead smoothed out.

"Her headache is gone," Serena told me.

Harriet didn't open her eyes at the sound of Serena's voice. I felt an excited flutter in my stomach. I really *was* the only one who could hear her.

Serena waved her hand again.

Harriet's bathwater started to bubble gently. The room was filled with the scent of fresh flowers.

Harriet looked delighted. She started to hum.

OK, so Serena could do some neat tricks. I even believed that she was my guardian angel. But that didn't mean she could help *me*. I didn't have a simple problem like a headache. My problems were serious.

CHAPTER 5
Serena's Story

"Why are you here?" I asked Serena when we got back to my room. I still didn't think I needed a guardian angel.

"To help you with your problems," Serena said. She went over to my dollhouse. "This is really neat."

"Thanks," I said. "What problems?"

Serena laughed. She had a beautiful laugh—like bells ringing. "Well, your parents are getting divorced. That's hard on any kid. And you also don't know what to do about Jessica and Elizabeth's cookie party."

My mouth dropped open. "You know about all that?"

"Of course," Serena said as she straightened up the chairs around my tiny dining-room set. "I'm always watching you."

"Always?"

Serena nodded firmly. "It's a good thing, too. If it hadn't been for me, you would have had a major fight with Jessica today."

"*You* stopped the fight?" I asked.

Serena grinned with delight. "Yup! I made Jessica forgive you. Didn't you see me?"

"I saw a white flash," I said.

"That was me!" Serena said. "Of course, Jessica and Eva didn't see the flash. Only you saw that."

"Well, thanks," I said.

"No problem," Serena said. "But, remember, nothing good comes from lying."

I sat down next to Serena on the

31

floor. I was beginning to change my mind about her. *Maybe she really can help me,* I thought.

"What should I do about the cookie party?" I asked.

"Tell the twins the truth about your mom," Serena said.

"I don't want to," I told her. "None of my friends' parents are divorced. They won't like me if I'm different."

Serena reached for my hand. My skin started to tingle where she touched me. Her face was very sad. "You *have* to tell your friends," she said. "I know. I learned the hard way."

"How?" I asked.

"When I was eight years old, I lived in this house. In fact, I lived right in this room, just like you do!"

I gasped. I had never known there was another little girl there before me. "Why don't you live here now?" I asked.

"Well, that year I found out I had a serious illness," Serena explained.

"Did you get better?" I asked.

"No," Serena said. "I died a few months later."

I felt a nervous tickle in my stomach. But Serena didn't seem sad.

"When I found out I was sick," Serena continued, "I didn't want to tell my friends. I was embarrassed. Even when I knew I was dying, I kept my secret. I was in the hospital for weeks. My family was with me, but I missed my friends. I was angry with them for not being there."

"But that's not fair," I said. "They didn't even know you were sick!"

"And your friends don't know you're sad," Serena said. "This is what I found out: You have to tell your friends the truth if you want them to help you. And that's why I'm here to help—because you live in my room and because you have a problem like mine. I'll do everything I can to cheer you up, Lila, but only your friends can really help. You have to tell them what's wrong."

I thought about that for a few minutes. "I'll try," I whispered. But I knew it wasn't going to be easy.

"Great," Serena said. "Since that's settled, we can play with your dollhouse now."

I smiled at her. Having Serena around was fun. I already felt less lonely.

CHAPTER 6
First Try

"This is going to be fun," Serena said as we walked into school together the next day. "I've already been in second grade. I'm going to know all the answers."

"Good, you can help me in spelling." I made a face. "That's my worst subject."

"OK," Serena said happily.

I was a little nervous about bringing an angel to school without permission. But, after all, Serena *was* invisible.

"Where are you going to sit?" I

asked as we walked into Mrs. Otis's room.

"I don't know," Serena said. "But don't worry about it."

"Maybe someone will be absent today," I said.

I went over to my desk to put my books away. Jessica and Elizabeth were sitting at their desks. Jessica was coloring her fingernails with a red marker. Elizabeth was reading a book.

"This is my desk," I told Serena.

Jessica gave me a funny look. "Who are you talking to?"

I covered my mouth with my hand. "Nobody," I said quickly.

"Go ahead and tell them about your parents," Serena said.

"Now?" I whispered.

"Why not?" Serena asked.

Elizabeth and Jessica looked at each other in surprise.

"Now *what?*" Jessica asked me.

I took a deep breath. "I have something to tell you. . . ." I looked at Serena, who nodded. "Um—Mommy can't come to your party."

"That's too bad," Elizabeth said.

"Is she sick?" Jessica asked.

Before I could explain, Lois Waller came up to us. "Hi, everybody," she said quietly.

I groaned. I didn't like Lois. She was chubby, and she still wore her hair in pigtails. She also used to be the biggest crybaby in the entire second grade.

Jessica rolled her eyes at me. She didn't like Lois, either.

But Elizabeth smiled at her. "Hi, Lois," she said in a friendly voice.

"Hi," Lois said. "My mom says we can come to your party. We even looked at the cookbook last night. We're going to make lemon squares."

"That's great," Elizabeth said. "We love lemon squares. Right, Jessica?"

"I guess," Jessica said.

"I've got to go finish my math problems," Lois said. "See you guys later."

After Lois had skipped off to her desk, I made a face. "Why did you invite *her* to the party?" I asked Jessica.

"Elizabeth wanted to invite everyone," Jessica said.

"I like Lois," Elizabeth added.

"I don't," I said.

Serena frowned at me, but I didn't pay any attention.

"Me neither," Jessica said.

Elizabeth looked angry. "Why not? She doesn't cry all the time like she used to. She's grown up a lot."

"She still wears baby clothes," Jessica said.

"And she's the only girl in our class

38

who wears her hair in pigtails," I added.

"So what?" Elizabeth asked.

Jessica shrugged. "She's just too . . . different."

The bell rang, and I slipped into my desk.

"That wasn't very nice," Serena told me.

I shrugged. I was sure that if Serena knew Lois better, she wouldn't like her, either.

Mrs. Otis started to take attendance.

Serena wandered over to look at our class hamsters, Tinkerbell and Thumbelina, and our class bunny. I wondered if *they* could see her.

Mrs. Otis wrote ten words on the blackboard. She asked us to write a sentence with each one.

"So why can't your mom come?" Jessica whispered to me after we had been working for a while.

"Um . . ." I was scared to tell Jessica the truth. She didn't like Lois because she was different. But wearing pigtails was nothing compared to having divorced parents.

"I'll tell you later," I whispered back.

"Jessica, Lila," Mrs. Otis said. "No whispering, please."

For once I was happy to follow Mrs. Otis's rules.

I was trying to think of a sentence with "succeed" in it when Serena came up to my desk.

"If at first you don't succeed, try, try again," Serena suggested.

That was a good sentence. "Thanks," I whispered very, very quietly.

"You're welcome," Serena said. "Are *you* going to try again?"

I nodded slowly.

Serena smiled at me. "You already told them your mom couldn't come. Telling them about the divorce shouldn't be too hard."

I wasn't so sure about that.

CHAPTER 7

Serena's Wings

"Let's play hopscotch!" Jessica suggested as she skipped out of the lunchroom ahead of Ellen and me.

Serena was following us. I was getting better at pretending she wasn't there. I had learned not to talk to her in front of my friends. But *she* still talked to *me*.

"Hopscotch sounds fun," Ellen agreed.

"It's my turn to go first," I added.

"No way," Ellen said. "You went first yesterday!"

"Did not!" I said.

Serena tapped me on the shoulder. "You left your purse in the lunchroom."

"Oh, no," I said. My pretty purple purse had a brand-new dollar bill in it. There was nothing to buy at school, but I liked to carry it around and show it off.

"Wait up, you guys!" I called after Ellen and Jessica. "I forgot my purse."

"We'll meet you out there!" Ellen called back.

I frowned. I didn't want Jessica and Ellen to start the game without me—I wanted to go first.

"Why didn't you tell me about my purse sooner?" I asked Serena in a crabby voice.

"Because I wanted to talk to you," Serena said as we hurried back into the lunchroom. "When are you going to tell them about the divorce?"

44

I groaned. Serena had already asked me that question about a hundred and three times. I'd been putting off telling my friends all morning. But I was getting tired of Serena nagging me. I wanted to get it over with.

"I'll do it on the playground," I promised her.

Serena grinned. "Really? That's great!"

When we got outside, I saw that all of the hopscotch boards were full. Jessica and Ellen were with a bunch of kids over by the jungle gym. They were all laughing loudly at something. Serena and I hurried over to see what was going on. Winston Egbert was at the center of the crowd. He was sitting at the bottom of the slide.

"If you open your presents on Christmas Eve, what do you do on

Christmas Day?" Ellen asked Winston in a nasty voice.

"We go to my grandmother's," Winston said with a shrug. "It's a long drive, so we have to start early in the morning."

Winston was skinny and his ears stuck out. He was always tripping over things and falling down. Ellen's big sister said that Winston was a nerd. My friends and I liked to tease him.

"What's going on?" I asked Jessica.

"Winston just told us his family opens their Christmas presents on Christmas Eve!" Jessica said with a laugh.

"Yeah, Winston is such a baby, he can't wait until the morning," Kisho Murasaki added.

Winston's face turned red. "I am not a baby. My family just does things a little differently, that's all."

I didn't see what the big deal was.

Sometimes it *is* hard to wait until Christmas morning to open presents. In a way, I thought Winston was lucky. But I couldn't say that. Everyone else thought he was weird.

"We *always* open our presents on Christmas Day," I said, sticking my nose in the air.

"Of course!" Ellen slipped her arm through mine. "*Your* family is normal."

When I heard that, my stomach took a swan dive. I couldn't tell my friends about the divorce now. If they made fun of Winston just for opening his presents early, imagine what they would say to me!

"When are you going to tell them?" Serena asked me for the two hundred and sixth time later that afternoon.

I was trying to think about the

math problems on my worksheet. I stuck my tongue out at her.

"Well?" Serena was standing right in front of my desk with her hands on her hips.

With a sigh, I raised my hand.

"Yes, Lila?" Mrs. Otis said.

"May I please go to the bathroom?" I asked.

"Of course," Mrs. Otis said.

I got up and grabbed the hall pass. I motioned for Serena to follow me down the hall. Luckily, the bathroom was empty when we got there.

As soon as the door closed behind us, I faced Serena squarely. "I can't do it," I told her firmly. "I'm never going to be able to do it."

"Are you sure?" Serena asked.

I nodded.

Serena looked sad. "I'll never get my wings now," she said.

"What?" I asked.

"Remember when I told you I hadn't got my wings yet?" Serena said.

"Sure," I said. "You also said you couldn't wait to fly."

Serena sighed. "Well, I'll never get to fly now. See, I was supposed to earn my wings by helping you. And I failed."

I felt terrible. Serena had been nice to me. I really liked her, and I wanted to help her. But I was still afraid to tell my friends about the divorce.

"What if you did a *different* good deed for me?" I suggested. "Something that had nothing to do with my friends? Would you get your wings then?"

Serena looked thoughtful. "Maybe . . ."

"If you think of another good deed to do, I promise to help you," I said. "Just as long as I don't have to tell my friends about the divorce."

"OK," Serena said finally. "I'm going to go back to your house to think."

"You're leaving?" I asked. Serena had been at my side ever since she'd appeared. It would be strange without her.

"Yeah," Serena said. "I'll see you later."

"OK," I agreed.

After Serena left, I felt lonely. I spent most of the afternoon trying to think of a good deed. I didn't want it to be my fault my guardian angel couldn't get her wings.

CHAPTER 8

Daddy and Me

"How was school today?" Harriet asked as I climbed into her funny little yellow car after school.

"Fine," I said. "What are you wearing?"

Harriet looked confused. She was dressed in jeans and a blue work shirt. Then she laughed. "Do you mean in my ears?"

"Yes!" I said with a giggle.

Harriet had on funny earrings— they looked like teensy-weensy candy canes.

"These are my special Christmas

earrings," Harriet told me. "I got them at the mall. The store had lots of fun ones—snowmen and tiny presents and Christmas stockings. Do you want to stop at the mall on the way home? Your dad told me you like to shop."

I almost said yes. But then I remembered Serena. "No, thanks," I said slowly.

"Are you sure?" Harriet asked, sounding disappointed. "You could have your snack there if you like."

I knew Harriet was trying to make friends with me. Even though I still didn't want a nanny, I had to admit she was nice. But I shook my head firmly. "No. I want to go home."

Harriet shrugged. "OK."

As soon as we got home, I ran up to my room.

"Hi!" Serena was sitting on the floor, playing with my dollhouse. She liked it the best of all my toys. She told me that she used to have one just like it.

"Hi!" It was fun having Serena waiting for me—it was almost like having a sister.

"I thought of another good deed to do," Serena announced. "I think I'm going to get my wings, after all."

"Great!" I said, joining Serena in front of the doll house. "What is it?"

"I'm going to fix things up between you and your father," Serena said.

"What do you mean?" I gave her an angry look. "Everything is fine between me and my father."

"No, it's not," Serena said softly. "You're mad at him for not spending more time with you."

I looked down at my lap. "That's true. . . ."

"Don't worry," Serena said. "I have a plan. First, you have to ask your father to help you make cookies."

"I don't—" I started.

"Lila, you *promised* you'd help me!" Serena interrupted.

I wanted to tell Serena it was hopeless. The only thing Daddy liked to do was work. He would never agree to make cookies. And that meant she would never get her wings.

"Will you do it?" Serena asked.

"OK," I said. At least when Daddy said no, it would be his fault Serena failed. Not mine.

"Let's go!" Serena said.

"Is Daddy home?" I asked.

Serena nodded. "He's in his study."

I was surprised. Daddy usually didn't come home until after dinner. I got up and brushed off my pants. "I'm ready," I said.

Serena and I went downstairs together.

Standing outside the closed door of

Daddy's study, I could feel my heart starting to beat faster. I wanted Daddy to say yes so badly. But I was pretty positive he would say no.

"Go ahead and knock," Serena said.

I took a deep breath and knocked very softly. I almost hoped Daddy wouldn't hear me.

"Come in!" he yelled.

I jumped about two feet into the air.

Serena was smiling. "Go in," she said.

I pushed open the heavy door. Serena and I went in together. Daddy was sitting behind his huge desk. Papers were piled everywhere. On the desk was a phone with lots of buttons and a computer with a big screen.

"Lila!" Daddy sounded surprised. "How was school today?"

I bit my lip. I didn't want to talk about school. I was too nervous to waste time.

"Daddy, will you help me bake cookies?" I asked quickly.

"Well . . ." Daddy scratched his chin.

"Right now," I added.

"Sure, why not?" Daddy said.

"What?" I was so surprised, I
thought I hadn't heard him right.

But Daddy was already getting to
his feet. "What kind of cookies would
you like to make?"

"Um—how about chocolate chip?" I
suggested.

"Those are my favorites," Daddy
said with a wink.

Daddy was actually going to make
cookies with me! I had never been so
surprised in my entire life. I was very
happy as we went into the kitchen
together.

Serena looked pleased with herself.

I was pleased with her, too.

Daddy rolled up his sleeves. He found
a bag of chocolate chips in the cabinet.

He read out the ingredients. I dashed around the kitchen finding them.

I was looking for the butter in the refrigerator when the phone rang.

"Fowler residence," Daddy said into the phone. "Oh, hi, Bert. Yes, yes. Mm-hmm. OK. I just need to look at some papers and I'll give you the answer. Hold on."

"Where are you going?" I asked Daddy as he headed for the kitchen door.

"Just into my study," he said. "I'll be right back."

"OK," I said.

Serena helped me find the butter. Then we sat down at the counter to wait for Daddy. After a few minutes, I got bored. Serena and I tried to read the recipe, but it was too hard for us. I opened the bag of chocolate chips and ate a few. They were yummy.

"What a long phone call," Serena complained.

I nodded. "Daddy can talk on the phone for *hours*. I hope he comes back soon."

The kitchen door swung open. Harriet came in. "Are you ready to make some cookies?" she asked me.

I frowned. "What happened to Daddy?"

"He had to go to the office," Harriet said. "Something important came up. But don't worry. I'm going to finish making the cookies with you."

Hot tears rushed to my eyes. I got up and ran out of the kitchen.

"Lila!" Harriet called after me.

"Lila!" Serena was calling, too.

But I didn't stop until I got to my room. Then I threw myself onto my bed and let the tears come. Serena was right—I *was* mad at Daddy. He never made time for me. Not even enough to tell me he was leaving.

CHAPTER 9

Serena's Recipe

"Lila?"

I buried my face deeper into my pillow. I didn't want to talk to Harriet or Serena. I was too upset.

"Hey, Lila, why are you crying?"

I recognized the voice and sat up in a hurry. "Jessica! What are you doing here?"

Jessica wiped a smudge of flour off her nose. "I came to get you."

"Why?" I asked.

"Well, I was baking cookies with my family," Jessica explained. "The recipe in our cookbook called for flour, butter, sugar, and a best friend to help stir."

"What a strange cookbook!" I said. And then I realized—Serena must have rewritten it. She must have zapped Jessica, too, because Jessica didn't seem to think anything was strange.

"Why were you crying?" Jessica asked again.

"Well, I . . ." I could have lied. But Jessica really did seem worried about me. If I was ever going to tell the truth, I had to do it now, while it was just the two of us.

I took a deep breath. "I'm upset about Mommy and Daddy."

"Did they have a fight?" Jessica asked.

"Kind of," I said. "Actually, they had lots of fights. They're getting a divorce."

Jessica sat down next to me on my bed. She didn't laugh or make fun of

me, like I was worried she might. "Why are they getting divorced?" she asked.

"Daddy said they don't love each other anymore," I explained. "They weren't happy living together. So Mommy moved out. She doesn't even live in Sweet Valley now. That's why she can't come to your party."

"I'm sorry," Jessica said. "You must be sad."

"I am," I admitted.

Jessica gave me a big hug. It felt very nice.

"Why don't you bring your dad to the party?" Jessica asked after the hug.

"He always has to work," I said glumly. "We didn't even get to make any cookies together."

"Then why don't you come bake cookies at my house?" Jessica suggested. "You can spend the night, and be a part of my family for as long as you want."

I thought that sounded great.

"Let me ask Harriet if I can go," I said.

"I'll come with you," Jessica said.

"No," I said quickly. "Um—it would be better if you stayed here."

Jessica shrugged. "OK."

I went out into the hallway and closed my bedroom door behind me. "Serena!" I whispered. "Serena—can you hear me?"

She didn't answer. *Where did she go?* I wondered.

I went down the hall to Harriet's room. She said it was fine for me to sleep over at Jessica's.

While I got ready to go, I wondered what had happened to Serena. I was worried about her. She knew her second good deed had failed. But did she know I had told Jessica the truth? That meant her first good deed was done, and she had earned her wings. I hoped she knew—and that she'd come back soon.

CHAPTER 10

Almost Like Triplets

Elizabeth took a deep breath and smiled. "I think the next batch is finished!"

Mrs. Wakefield peeked into the oven. "You're right," she told Elizabeth. "You have a good nose."

"And I have gooey fingers!" Jessica held up her fingers, which were covered with green icing. She started to lick them clean. "Yummy!"

Jessica, Elizabeth, and I were sitting at the Wakefields' kitchen table. When the cookies came out of the oven, they were just plain sugar cookies. Our job was to cover them with red, green, and white icing, raisins, nuts, and sprinkles, until each one looked like a tiny Santa Claus.

"This is my best one yet!" Elizabeth announced, holding up her latest creation.

Elizabeth hadn't noticed that her big brother, Steven, was sneaking up behind her. Steven snatched the cookie out of Elizabeth's hand and bit off Santa's head.

"Steven!" Elizabeth yelled. "I wanted my friends to see that tomorrow."

"Want it back?" Steven asked, holding out the half-eaten cookie.

Elizabeth sighed. "No. I'll make another one."

Still munching, Steven bent over to examine the cookies we had decorated. "Yours are really nice, Lila," he said.

"Thank you," I said. Usually Steven

was a big pain. But he was being very nice to me tonight.

"That's the last batch," Mrs. Wakefield announced. She put the cookies that had just come out of the oven on the table.

"Goody!" Jessica said. "I'm getting tired of decorating. We must have made about a thousand cookies already."

"Feels like it," Mrs. Wakefield agreed.

"We made something else, too," Elizabeth said. "A mess!"

We all laughed.

The Wakefields' kitchen *was* a wreck. There were dirty mixing bowls, spoons, and cookie sheets all mixed in with bags of flour, sugar, measuring spoons, and lots of other stuff.

Jessica carefully smoothed red icing over a plain cookie. "At least the rest of the house is ready for the party," she said.

That was true. Earlier, the twins and I had helped Mr. Wakefield clean and decorate the house. We had vacuumed and dusted and scrubbed. Then we had put a pretty red tablecloth on the dining-room table and strung up crepe paper. We had a big bag of balloons to blow up the next morning. The Wakefields' house wasn't nearly as fancy as mine, but it looked nice.

"Why don't you girls finish up that last batch?" Mrs. Wakefield suggested. "Then you can get ready for bed while I clean up."

"After we get ready, can we watch TV?" Jessica asked.

Mrs. Wakefield nodded. "Maybe a Christmas special is on tonight."

A few minutes later Elizabeth, Jessica, and I had finished the cookies and changed into our pj's. We settled on the couch in the den. Mr. and Mrs. Wakefield and Steven were all there, too.

I felt sleepy and cozy. A movie called *It's a Wonderful Life* was on TV. There was an angel in the movie who reminded me of Serena. She still hadn't shown up. I missed her.

When a commercial came on, Mr. Wakefield reached over and tickled our feet. "I feel like I have triplets tonight," he said.

Jessica and Elizabeth giggled.

I smiled. All of the Wakefields were being extra nice to me. But I still felt unhappy. The twins got to live with their mom. Why didn't I? The twins' dad paid attention to them. Why didn't mine? It didn't seem fair.

CHAPTER 11

Cookies!

"What kind of cookies are these?" Todd Wilkins asked at the party the next day. A bunch of kids from my class were gathered around the huge display of cookies on the Wakefields' dining-room table. The adults were chatting in little groups.

"Those are jam tarts," Winston Egbert said. "Dad and I made them."

Elizabeth looked at the plate of cookies more carefully. "I don't see any jam."

Winston wrinkled his nose. "They didn't come out so well," he admitted.

"Dad and I went outside to play catch while they were cooking. We sort of forgot about them, and the jam ran out."

Todd popped a jam tart into his mouth. "They still taste good. You can hardly tell they're burned."

Yuck! Jessica and I looked at each other and giggled.

We were still laughing when Caroline Pearce and her mother came up. Caroline was wearing a fancy pink dress with matching bows in her hair. She always dresses in prissy clothes.

"Hello, Lila," Mrs. Pearce said. "Is your mother here? I haven't seen her."

Jessica rolled her eyes.

"She couldn't come," I mumbled.

"You're here all alone?" Mrs. Pearce was just as nosy as Caroline!

I nodded.

"You poor baby," Mrs. Pearce cooed.

I felt like kicking her. I didn't like being the only kid at the party without a parent. And I *definitely* didn't need Mrs. Pearce rubbing it in.

Just then the doorbell rang.

Mrs. Wakefield opened the door. "George!" she exclaimed. "What a nice surprise."

George is Daddy's first name. I spun around. Sure enough, Daddy was standing at the door! I was amazed. I hadn't even told him about the party!

"Daddy!" I yelled, running over to him. "What are you doing here?"

"Hi, sweetie," Daddy said. "How are the cookies?"

"Great," I said.

Daddy took my hand. "Come on, then. I want you to show me which ones are your favorites."

I led Daddy over to the table full of cookies. I warned him to stay away from the jam tarts. He selected several cookies—including one of the Santas I had decorated.

Daddy sat down on the couch and balanced his plate of cookies on his knee. I sat next to him.

Jessica ran up to us. "We're going outside," she told me. "Do you want to come?"

"I'll be out later," I told her.

"OK," Jessica agreed.

"How did you find out about the party?" I asked Daddy.

"Well, I had a very strange day," he explained with a puzzled expression. "First of all, the computer in my study kept turning itself off."

"Really?" I asked.

Daddy nodded. "I tried to call a repairman. But loud music was playing on my telephone. The repairman couldn't hear a word I said."

"That's weird," I said.

"I thought so, too," Daddy said. "But since I couldn't do anything else, I decided to read my mail. That's when I found the invitation on my desk."

"It was on your desk?" I asked.

Daddy nodded. His mouth was full.

Something about what he had said bothered me. I was sure I had left the invitation in my room. In fact, the whole story was odd. Computers don't turn themselves off!

I could think of only one explanation—Serena. For the four hundred and twelfth time I looked around for her. She was nowhere to be seen.

"Why didn't you tell me about the party?" Daddy asked.

"I didn't think you'd come," I said.

"Why not?" Daddy asked.

"Because you're always too busy for me," I said.

"That's not true!" Daddy exclaimed.

"Is so," I said. "Remember what happened yesterday? You left right in the middle of making cookies—without even telling me you were going!"

"Why didn't you want to make cookies with Harriet?" Daddy asked.

I thought for a moment. "I like Harriet. She's nice, and her hair is pretty. But I wanted to make cookies with you. You're my daddy—not Harriet."

Daddy looked sorry. "I guess I have a lot to learn about being a good parent," he said softly. "But, from now on, I promise to be there when you need me. You know I love you, don't you?"

"I guess," I whispered.

Daddy took my hand. "Well, I do love you. More than anything else in the world."

I smiled at him. I felt much better. Serena had been right all along. I wasn't alone. My friends didn't care if I was different. And Daddy loved me.

CHAPTER 12

Sort of Good-bye

After our talk, Winston's dad came up and asked Daddy about something boring. I went out into the backyard to try and find the other kids.

"Serena!" I exclaimed. She was standing in the middle of the Wakefields' backyard. She had a big grin on her face. "Where have you been? I've been looking for you all over."

"I just came back to say good-bye," Serena told me.

"Good-bye?" I repeated.

Serena nodded. "You don't need me anymore."

I was sad. But I knew Serena was right. I didn't need my guardian angel with me anymore. I had my dad and my friends.

"Will I ever see you again?" I asked Serena.

"If you ever need me, I'll be here," Serena said. "I promise."

I bit my lip so I wouldn't cry—but it was too late.

"Don't cry," Serena said. "Everything is going to be fine."

"I—I know," I said through my tears.

"I wish I could stay," Serena said. "But there are other kids who need my help."

"I understand," I said.

"Good-bye," Serena said.

" 'Bye," I whispered.

Serena waved as she started to walk across the grass.

I remembered something. "Hey, Serena—what about your wings?"

Serena didn't seem to hear me. But I still got my answer. Slowly and gracefully, Serena lifted off the ground—and flew away! Her beautiful, sparkling white wings stretched out behind her. I was very happy she had got her wings at last.

I watched Serena fly farther and farther away until she looked like a tiny speck in the sky. Just as that speck disappeared, Jessica, Ellen, Elizabeth, and Amy came galloping around the house. They were pretending to be horses. I knew Elizabeth and Amy must have thought up that game. They both take riding lessons—and they're horse crazy.

Elizabeth pretended to neigh as they all galloped up to me.

Amy pulled on her pretend reins.

"Where's your dad?" Ellen asked. I'd told her about the divorce earlier.

She didn't make fun of me any more than Jessica did.

"Inside," I said.

"I'm glad he came," Jessica said.

"Me, too," I said. "What are you guys doing?"

Amy galloped around in a circle. "Practicing for the horse show!"

"I'm going to be in it, too," Elizabeth announced.

"Not me," Jessica said with a giggle. "I only like *pretend* horses. The real ones smell."

Ellen sat down in the grass. "I wish I could be in the horse show. I'd like to win a blue ribbon."

"Me, too," Elizabeth said.

"Me, three!" Amy said.

Will Amy and Elizabeth do well in the horse show? Find out in Sweet Valley Kids #64, ELIZABETH'S HORSEBACK ADVENTURE.

SIGN UP FOR THE SWEET VALLEY HIGH® FAN CLUB!

Hey, girls! Get all the gossip on Sweet Valley High's® most popular teenagers when you join our fantastic Fan Club! As a member, you'll get all of this really cool stuff:

- Membership Card with your own personal Fan Club ID number
- A Sweet Valley High® Secret Treasure Box
- Sweet Valley High® Stationery
- Official Fan Club Pencil (for secret note writing!)
- Three Bookmarks
- A "Members Only" Door Hanger
- Two Skeins of J. & P. Coats® Embroidery Floss with flower barrette instruction leaflet
- Two editions of *The Oracle* newsletter
- Plus exclusive Sweet Valley High® product offers, special savings, contests, and much more!

- -

Be the first to find out what Jessica & Elizabeth Wakefield are up to by joining the Sweet Valley High® Fan Club for the one-year membership fee of only $6.25 each for U.S. residents, $8.25 for Canadian residents (U.S. currency). Includes shipping & handling.

Send a check or money order (do not send cash) made payable to "Sweet Valley High® Fan Club" along with this form to:

SWEET VALLEY HIGH® FAN CLUB, BOX 3919-B, SCHAUMBURG, IL 60168-3919

NAME_____
(Please print clearly)

ADDRESS_____

CITY_____ STATE _____ ZIP_____
(Required)

AGE_____BIRTHDAY_____ /_____ /_____

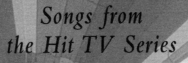

Songs from the Hit TV Series

Featuring:

"Rose Colored Glasses"

"Lotion"

"Sweet Valley High Theme"

Available on CD and Cassette Wherever Music is Sold.